W9-AOE-859

12/2015

A Beginning-to-Read Book

Dear Dragon Learns to Read

by Margaret Hillert

Illustrated by Jack Pullan

NORWOOD HOUSE PRESS

DEAR CAREGIVER, The *Beginning-to-Read* series is a carefully written collection of classic readers you may remember from your own childhood. Each book features text comprised of common sight words to provide your child ample practice reading the words that appear most frequently in written text. The many additional details in the pictures enhance the story and offer the opportunity for you to help your child expand oral language and develop comprehension.

Begin by reading the story to your child, followed by letting him or her read familiar words and soon your child will be able to read the story independently. At each step of the way, be sure to praise your reader's efforts to build his or her confidence as an independent reader. Discuss the pictures and encourage your child to make connections between the story and his or her own life. At the end of the story, you will find reading activities and a word list that will help your child practice and strengthen beginning reading skills.

Above all, the most important part of the reading experience is to have fun and enjoy it!

Shannon Cannon

Shannon Cannon, Ph.D.
Literacy Consultant

Norwood House Press • P.O. Box 316598 • Chicago, Illinois 60631
For more information about Norwood House Press please visit our website at
www.norwoodhousepress.com or call 866-565-2900.

LIBRARY OF CONGRESS CATALOGING-IN-PUBLICATION DATA
   Hillert, Margaret.
    Dear Dragon learns to read / by Margaret Hillert ; illustrated by Jack Pullan.
     pages cm. -- (A Beginning-to-read book)
    Summary: "A boy and his pet dragon learn how to read. Together they help each other read, followed by a trip to the library for more books. This title includes reading activities and a word list"-- Provided by publisher.
    ISBN 978-1-59953-707-8 (library edition : alk. paper) --
    ISBN 978-1-60357-797-7 (ebook)
    [1. Reading--Fiction. 2. Dragons--Fiction.] I. Pullan, Jack, illustrator.II. Title.
    PZ7.H558Dei 2015
    [E]--dc23
                2014043665

275N–062015
Manufactured in the United States of America in Stevens Point, Wisconsin.

Today is a good day.
Today we will read to Dear Dragon.
He will like that.

I do not know how to read.

We will help you.
You can do it.

Look here.
I will read this to you.
This is fun.

Oh, yes.
I can read it.

This is fun.
Look at the pictures.

Can I read now?
Please let me do it.

You can read with a friend.
That is a good thing to do.

Yes, yes.
That is a good thing.

Now we will take this good book home, and I will read it to Mother and Father. They will be happy.

Mother...
Father...
I can READ!!
This is how I do it.

I will read to my dog, Spot.

I will read to my bear.

One, two, three.
One is the father.
One is the mother.
One is the baby.

I will read to Dear Dragon.

Reading is fun.
I wish we had more books.

Let's go to the library and
get some more books.
Come on.
Come on.

Oh Father, what a good spot.
Look at all the books.

READ

CHECK OUT

23

I want this —
And this.
And this.
Here is one that looks like you.

I cannot wait to read all of these books with Dear Dragon.

Here you are with me.
And here I am with you.
Oh what fun it is to read, Dear Dragon.

The following activities support the findings of the National Reading Panel that determined the most effective components for reading instruction are: Phonemic Awareness, Phonics, Vocabulary, Fluency, and Text Comprehension.

Phonemic Awareness: The /r/ sound

Sound Substitution: Say the words on the left to your child. Ask your child to repeat the word, changing the first sound to /**r**/:

lead = read	can = ran	cat = rat
night = right	not = rot	bed = red
want = rant	ate = rate	best = rest

Phonics: The letter Rr

1. Demonstrate how to form the letters **R** and **r** for your child.

2. Have your child practice writing **R** and **r** at least 3 times each.

3. Ask your child to point to the words in the book that start with the letter **r**.

4. Write down the following words and ask your child to circle the letter **r** in each word:

read	dear	dragon	here	more
library	picture	friend	mother	father
bear	start	rug	cart	

Vocabulary: Verbs

1. Explain to your child that words that describe actions are called verbs.

2. Write the following verbs on separate pieces of paper:

read	go	look	get	see	help

3. Randomly place the pieces of paper on a flat surface. Read each verb to your child and ask your child to repeat it. Then, point to a word and ask your child to read it.

4. Read the following sentences to your child. Ask your child to provide an appropriate verb to complete the sentence.

   • I'm bored! Let's (read) with our friends.

   • I need to finish reading this book before I (go) to school tomorrow.

   • Reading is so fun! I like to (help) others learn how to read.

   • Would you like to (get) a book from the library?

   • Will you help me (look) for this book? I do not (see) what I am looking for.

Fluency: Echo Reading

1. Reread the story to your child at least two more times while your child tracks the print by running a finger under the words as they are read. Ask your child to read the words he or she knows with you.

2. Reread the story, stopping after each sentence or page to allow your child to read (echo) what you have read. Repeat echo reading and let your child take the lead.

Text Comprehension: Discussion Time

1. Ask your child to retell the sequence of events in the story.

2. To check comprehension, ask your child the following questions:

   • Books have words, but what other things can you see in a book?

   • Who can you practice reading with?

   • If you want more books to read, where can you go to find more books?

   • What is your favorite book to practice reading?

WORD LIST

Dear Dragon Learns to Read uses the **73** words listed below.

The **6** words bolded below serve as an introduction to new vocabulary, while the other 67 are pre-primer. You may wish to write the words on index cards and use them to help your child build automatic word recognition. Regular practice with these words will enhance your child's fluency in reading connected text.

a	father	know	**pictures**	wait
all	friend		please	want
am	fun	let		we
and		let's	**read**	what
are	get	**library**	**reading**	will
at	go	like		wish
	good	look(s)	some	with
be			spot	
bear	had	me		yes
book(s)	happy	more	take	you
	he	mother	that	
can	help	my	the	
cannot	here		these	
come	home	not	they	
	how	now	thing	
day			this	
dear	I	of	to	
do	is	oh	today	
dog	it	on		
dragon		one		

ABOUT THE AUTHOR Margaret Hillert has written over 80 books for children who are just learning to read. Her books have been translated into many different languages and over a million children throughout the world have read her books. She first started writing poetry as a child and has continued to write for children and adults throughout her life. A first grade teacher for 34 years, Margaret is now retired from teaching and lives in Michigan where she likes to write, take walks in the morning, and care for her three cats.

Photograph by Glenna Washburn

ABOUT THE ILLUSTRATOR A talented and creative illustrator, Jack Pullan, is a graduate of William Jewell College. He has also studied informally at Oxford University and the Kansas City Art Institute. He was mentored by the renowned watercolor artists, Jim Hamil and Bill Amend. Jack's work has graced the pages of many enjoyable children's books, various educational materials, cartoon strips, as well as many greeting cards. Jack currently resides in Kansas.